LOOK AND FIND®

Disney's
THE WILD

Illustrated by Art Mawhinney
Written by Amanda Barnett

Published by Louis Weber, C.E.O., Publications International, Ltd.
7373 North Cicero Avenue, Lincolnwood, Illinois 60712

Ground Floor, 59 Gloucester Place, London W1U 8JJ

www.pilbooks.com

Look and Find is a registered trademark of
Publications International, Ltd.

p i kids is a registered trademark of Publications International, Ltd.

8 7 6 5 4 3 2 1
ISBN 1-4127-6088-7

publications international, ltd.

Ryan, Duke, and Eze have spooked the gazelles — and now they've stampeded into the curling championship! Can you find these characters in the chaos?

Donald

Victor

This gazelle

Duke

Eze

Monkey girls

Everyone knows that sewers aren't clean, but this is ridiculous! Sift through the trash to find these items:

Motel key

Accordion

Tube of toothpaste

Love letters

False teeth

Map

Ryan's friends are trying to find him before he is shipped to the Wild! Help them search, and see if you can find these other New York exports:

Search the talented wildebeests' lair for these items that help support their musical theater habit.

White gloves

Tap shoes

Record album

Autographed photograph

Top hat and cane

Costume with sequins

Samson is lost, but the chameleons are helping him find his way. Can you spot these unusual landmarks they've created?

Polka-dot leaves

Plaid rock

Yellow brick path

Zig-zag bush

Pink arrow

Striped tree trunk

Samson realizes he shouldn't have hidden his past from Ryan and his friends. Go back in time to the big top to look for these performers:

Elephant

Boa Constrictor

Tiger

Horse

Monkey

Bear

The gang is going home, and they're taking their new friends along. Can you find them in the crowd?

Cloak

This wildebeest

Hyrax

This wildebeest

Camo

Blag

CATNIP

Revisit the zoo to find the tourists enjoying these tasty snacks:

☐ Lollipop
☐ Red licorice rope
☐ Popcorn
☐ Cotton candy
☐ Ice-cream cone
☐ Hot dog

Attend the curling championship and scout out these stadium sights:

☐ Megaphone
☐ "#1 Fan" foam finger
☐ Samson pennant
☐ Penguin hats
☐ Fish-head vendor
☐ Turtle balloon

Slink back to the sewer to locate these treasures:

☐ Diamond ring
☐ Penny jar
☐ Stamp collection
☐ Wristwatch
☐ Suitcase stuffed with money
☐ Safe

Sail back to the dock and make sure everything is shipshape by finding these items:

☐ Boat captain
☐ Life preserver
☐ Tugboat
☐ Seagull
☐ Anchor
☐ Coil of rope

Leap back to the volcano chamber and look for these wildebeests dancing to their own beat:

- ❑ Break-dancing wildebeest
- ❑ Ballroom-dancing wildebeests
- ❑ Ballerina wildebeest
- ❑ Square-dancing wildebeests
- ❑ Head-banging wildebeest
- ❑ Hula-dancing wildebeest

Swing back to the jungle and search for these tropical fruits:

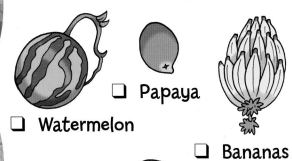

- ❑ Watermelon
- ❑ Papaya
- ❑ Bananas
- ❑ Mango
- ❑ Pineapple
- ❑ Coconut

Return to the circus and see if you can spot these other star performers:

- ❑ Clown on a tricycle
- ❑ Trapeze artist
- ❑ Organist
- ❑ Ringmaster
- ❑ Sword juggler
- ❑ Tightrope walker

Swim back to the last scene to find these sea creatures:

- ❑ Shark
- ❑ Catfish
- ❑ Swordfish
- ❑ Puffer fish
- ❑ Dolphin
- ❑ Whale

EXTRA CHALLENGE
Try to find at least one Nigel the "I Like You" koala doll in every scene!

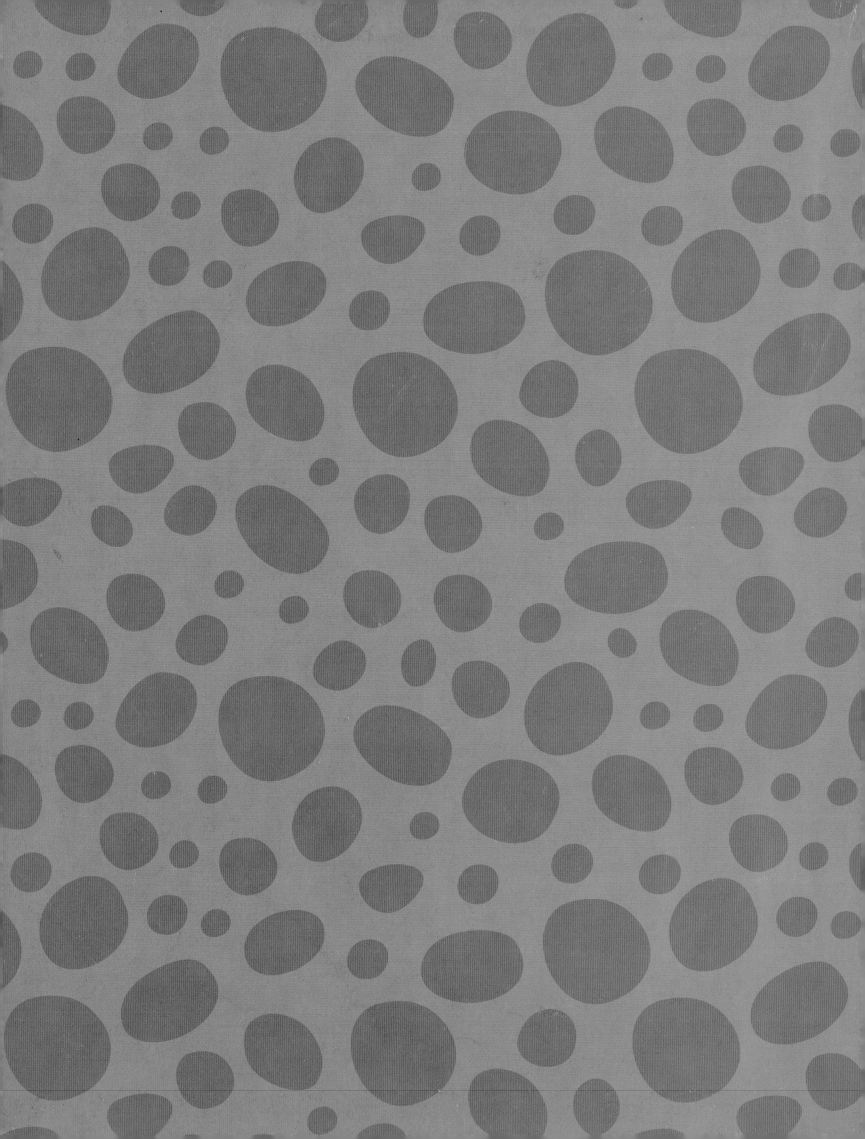